The ADVENTURES of Big Al

A Collection of unbelievable short stories

C.L. Adams

LifeRich
PUBLISHING

This is a work of fiction. All of the characters, names, incidents, organizations, and dialogue in this novel are either the products of the author's imagination or are used fictitiously.

LifeRich Publishing is a registered trademark of The Reader's Digest Association, Inc.

LifeRich Publishing books may be ordered through booksellers or by contacting:

LifeRich Publishing
1663 Liberty Drive
Bloomington, IN 47403
www.liferichpublishing.com
1 (888) 238-8637

Because of the dynamic nature of the Internet, any web addresses or links contained in this book may have changed since publication and may no longer be valid. The views expressed in this work are solely those of the author and do not necessarily reflect the views of the publisher, and the publisher hereby disclaims any responsibility for them.

ISBN: 978-1-4897-2656-8 (sc)
ISBN: 978-1-4897-2681-0 (e)

Library of Congress Control Number: 2020908410

Print information available on the last page.

LifeRich Publishing rev. date: 05/27/2020

I dedicate this book to Big Al, who's friendship means so much, who has supported me every step of the way throughout this process, and who's stories throughout the years of friendship have inspired this book.

I dedicate this book to my husband Peter, who has endured the nightstand light being on passed 'lights out.'

PREFACE

Before we delve into the "meat" of the book, I think it's imperative to give a little insight into Big Al. There are people in our lives that are very predictable, and that you can describe in just a few words. There are people that you just know who they are, and what they're all about. And then there's Big Al, who'll surprise you just when you think you've got him pegged.

Big Al was a very rambunctious kid and needed to stay active. He enjoyed playing all types of sports; baseball, football, soccer, hockey. When he wasn't playing in an organized sport, Big Al and his brother were constantly roughhousing. One day, during yet another (unofficial) wrestling match with his brother, Big Al's dad insisted that they sign up for boxing or something. Big Al's dad knew someone from work, who taught Martial Arts on the side from his home, and after talking with Big Al's dad, he agreed to give Big Al private lessons.

Since his very first lesson, Martial Arts became Big Al's passion. No matter what else he had going on, Martial Arts was always a part of his daily routine. The first time he took a class, he knew this form of art would somehow shape his life. Those lessons ignited a flame in him, and he grew into the expert that he is today. When Big Al's neighbor was no longer able to give him lessons, he went to the only other school that did in Morristown, NJ. I'm telling you this because even though I'm sure you will *enjoy* the stories that follow, to truly *appreciate* the rest of the book, I think it's important to understand that Martial Arts is not only something that Big Al does, but is a big part of who he is. The principles on which the art are based, are evident in how he lives his life: Working with what you have, being flexible, (both physically and mentally), being adaptable to your surroundings, being aware of your surroundings, but knowing that anything could happen, and making the most out of each moment. These are just a few examples.

Big Al has many layers to his personality, but fun is present in every facet. It may be that the situation naturally gives way to fun, but if not, Big Al will find a way to manifest the fun himself, somehow.

Even before he could speak, Big Al loved to make people laugh. He prides himself on it. And he always finds himself in situations that are contusive to humor. With Big Al, one could always expect the unexpected. The element of surprise has become his all-time favorite concept to master.

FOREWORD

I met Big Al many years ago through my best friend Peter, who was looking to go to Big Al's Martial Arts school. Big Al's school is further from us than other schools, but Big Al's reputation as a world class instructor preceded him, and Peter wanted the best. I thought this would be the extent of our relationship, but I was sorely mistaken. I didn't think we'd become such good friends, but every time I have gotten together with Big Al, he has astounded me, showing me a different side of him, and the special person he is. In all the years I've known Big Al, I have never walked away from a meeting with him without at least laughing once or twice.

During our friendship, Big Al has shared with me many stories, some serious and very interesting, and some, still very interesting, but they had me laughing so loud that other people that weren't in the same conversation would turn their heads. In this book, I am going to focus on his lighter side.

I'm sure you will enjoy the following stories, laughing throughout as you turn the pages.

HEAD CHIMP

When Big Al came home one night in 1977 from being out with some friends, his house was very calm and quiet. In fact, the only movement was that of his mother who came to the kitchen for a glass of water. There was a slight chill in the air for the middle of August, but it was a welcoming break from the blistering heat of daytime. Still, even though the air conditioner was on full blast it didn't seem to be enough.

The calm and quiet didn't last for long; Big Al and his mom were just hanging out in the kitchen, talking about their days, when suddenly, they heard noises coming from outside. Their house was not near a busy street, so the noise had to be coming from something else. Big Al and his mom went outside to see what the ruckus was about. They found an unexpected, but not unusual, surprise. Big Al's Uncle Fred and Cousin John had come to visit, and they brought some friends- the wild animals they housed, took care of, and trained to perform stunts in circuses and movies.

Uncle Fred and Cousin John lived in California, but they traveled to all different states with their animals. Whenever they came to New Jersey, they would come to Big Al's house for a visit. And along with them came the dozens of trailers filled with all kinds of animals-giraffes, camels, horses, elephants, rhinos, etc. These animals were certainly not considered pets, except one. Buddy, the Chimpanzee spent all his spare time with the family. Whenever Buddy wasn't performing, he was in the house, or wherever the family was to be found. The two weeks visiting with Big Al and his family were no different. Buddy often found himself roughhousing with Big Al and John in the family room or outside in the yard.

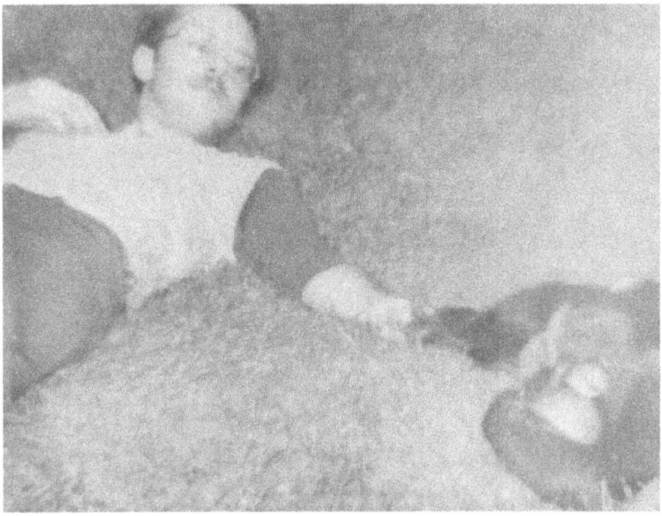

Buddy's favorite part of that visit, though, was the daily trips he took with Big Al down to the local seven-eleven. Buddy's favorite treat was a frozen soda, but, just like a kid, he would grab whatever was within his reach as he and Big Al made their way to the frozen soda aisle. Unlike a kid though, his large, strong hand would crush anything he reached for, so there was no putting it back. By the time Buddy and Big Al left, Buddy's face was covered in twinkies, and chocolate, and, of course, he was sipping on his frozen coke. Big Al would never had suspected what was about to happen. No one would.

Uncle Fred and John were at Big Al's for a couple of weeks. Fun was always on the agenda during the stay. Every other day seemed like one big party for the whole neighborhood. Uncle Fred and John spent much of their time giving rides to the neighbors on elephants, giraffes, and horses. One day, during yet another massive BBQ, everyone was enjoying themselves, riding animals, eating, having great conversations, and just having a good summer day.

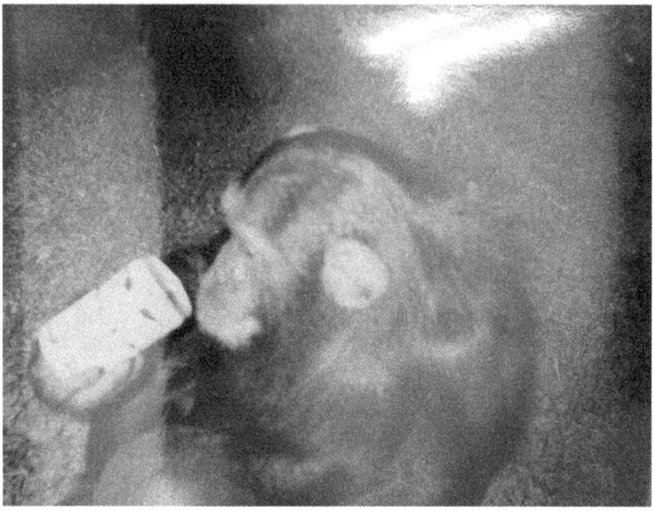

Big Al and Buddy were playing in the front yard. Buddy would run around the yard for a bit, then come up to Big Al. Big Al would then roll him up like a ball and toss him into the front yard. Buddy would run around again, then come back so Big Al could roll him again. This play went on for a while.

The last time Buddy came back to Big Al did not turn out to be as playful as the others, though. Buddy came to Big Al, but Big Al was in the middle of a conversation with a couple of his neighbors. During the conversation, instead of rolling Buddy on the ground, Big Al would pet him on the head occasionally. Buddy did not like that!

Big Al was just sitting there on his front porch, he had his hand on his knee, and he was just talking. When all of a sudden, Buddy decided to wrap his mouth around Big Al's forearm! Buddy grabbed Big Al's arm with both hands and in an instant clamped down with his teeth, like he was biting into a nice juicy rib!! Big Al was taken by surprise and reacted by punching Buddy so hard in the nose that Buddy was thrown back. As he flew backwards, his teeth scraped along Big Al's forearm, leaving Big Al bleeding profusely. Even though Big Al's choice would have been to tend to his wounds, Buddy had other things in mind. He only allowed Big Al a split second to register the injury before he charged toward Big Al again. Big Al grabbed Buddy by his biceps, trying to keep him at a safe distance. Buddy was going nuts shrieking and trying to break free of Big Al's firm hold, making all kinds of chimp noises. Buddy then used his feet to claw at Big Al's neck and face. Big Al, in an attempt to escape the attack, threw Buddy to the ground. Buddy instantly bounces back up like the ground was a trampoline and lunges at Big Al once again with even more persistence than before. Big Al grabs him by the arms again and pins him to the ground, repeatedly punching him, hoping to hurt him just enough so that Buddy would stop. Unfortunately for Big Al, it's not that easy to hurt a chimp. Being made up of all muscle and 0% fat, a human can outswim one, but defeating them in a fist fight is impossible. Actually, hitting him just gets Buddy more riled up. Big Al was able to get in an uppercut, throwing Buddy back a way.

At this point everybody at the gathering had scattered, rightfully so. Big Al would rather be somewhere else, too. He could see the front door. It was only a couple of feet away, but it seemed like "looking through binoculars the wrong way." For a split second, Big Al wondered if he could make a run for it, but he knew that Buddy would be right on his back if he tried. Big Al realized that the only way out of this was to fight.

Once Buddy got back on his feet, he no longer looked like that cute little chimp, but rather like a shorter version of King Kong ready to pounce. He was circling Big Al, pounding the ground, once again baring those large carnivore teeth, fur puffed out, and staring at Big Al. Buddy somehow appeared taller. He charges towards Big Al, and instinct just kicks in. Big Al times it just right so that when Buddy leaps for him, Big Al grabs his upper arms, hurls him over his head, goes into a backwards roll, and slams

Buddy, headfirst, as hard as he could into the ground. Big Al hears a crack and thinks that Buddy would be out cold.

But Buddy was not out; when Big Al turned around, Buddy was just standing there, his arms over his head, his hands totally limp, staring at Big Al. Big Al, all torn up and bleeding, thought to himself, "what now?!" In that moment, John had gotten the other neighbors to safety, and had come back to see what he could do to help Big Al. John saw Buddy's stance and explained that this was a chimpanzee's way of admitting defeat. John tells Big Al that it is safe to approach Buddy now. Big Al turns to John, "Are you fucking crazy?!, I'm not going near that thing!!!" John laughs a little, and says, "I know, but really, it's ok." Big Al says, "well, ok, but if he goes nuts again, I'm coming after you!" Big Al *cautiously* walks up to Buddy, takes him by the hand, and leads him into the house.

Big Al then goes to nurse his wounds. He comes out of the bathroom all banged up, looking like he just came out of WWII, and what does he find? Buddy just calmly sitting in the family room, watching the Flintstones, and eating a bowl of dried Cheerios like nothing happened!

WHO'S FOOLING WHO?

Buddy, a young but good size chimpanzee, was not afraid of very much. Ironically, though, a small toy could always get the best of him. This toy was a little plastic Godzilla statue, and every time Buddy would encounter it, he would swat at it and then run around, making noises, warning everyone that there was danger amidst. Big Al would definitely be using this to his advantage.

After the "Head Chimp" incident, Big Al was all banged up, but he patched himself up and then went back outside to join his friends and neighbors in the festivities. After about 20 minutes, Big Al came back in to find Buddy still sitting there watching his Flintstones program. Big Al was amazed at how Buddy could turn on and off like a light switch; Buddy was so calm now, just like nothing had ever happened.

In that instant, Big Al thought of the plastic Godzilla, and thought it would be fun to get Buddy back! He went upstairs to get the toy. At the top of the stairs was a Dutch door, which led into Big Al's bedroom. He got the toy and stood it on the step at the halfway point of the staircase. He then went into his room and closed the bottom half of the Dutch door, leaving the top slightly ajar so that he could call Buddy. When Buddy heard his name, he went in the direction he thought the call was coming from.

At the bottom of the staircase was the front door, and since Big Al's voice was coming from that general area, Buddy went to the front door first, thinking that maybe someone outside wanted him, but there was no one there. Buddy turns to see Big Al at the top of the stairs. Buddy starts to run to him, but when he gets to the step where the Godzilla statue is, he swings at it so that it tilts over to its side, runs back down the stairs as fast as he can, and runs around the house making all kinds of noises.

Big Al calls out again, in a much softer voice this time and hiding behind the closed bottom door. Buddy goes back to look out the door, but no one is there, and he can't see Big Al. Now, Buddy's going crazy downstairs, back and forth to the front door and all-around downstairs. Big Al is laughing up a storm, hearing all the hustle and bustle, and continues to taunt Buddy by calling his name, then ducking behind the door so Buddy couldn't see him. Buddy knew somebody was calling him, but he couldn't figure out where the call was coming from at first.

Big Al continues to laugh uncontrollably. Experiencing the Buddy from "Head Chimp", to then witnessing this Buddy being so scared of a little toy was too much! Big Al keeps calling out for Buddy. Buddy finally sees Big Al but is so afraid of that little toy that he won't go up the stairs. Buddy doesn't give up, though. His goal is to get up those steps somehow, so he climbs up from the outside of the banister. Once he reaches the top, he just sits there, right outside Big Al's door. Big Al cracks the top portion again to taunt Buddy some more, but instead, finds Buddy just staring at him. The area between the top of the staircase and the door which Big Al was behind was very small, so until Buddy went down, Big Al was trapped! Big Al closes the door again and waits a little while longer without making a sound, in hopes that Buddy will get bored and go back downstairs. But Buddy refuses go back down the stairs because the Godzilla statue is still there. Luckily, Big Al's bedroom window was right above the festivities, so Big Al yelled out, "hey John, come get that stupid Godzilla toy off the steps so scardy-cat Buddy will move, and I can get outta here!"

KNOCK, KNOCK...

Everyone knows the saying, *the circus is coming to town.* Well, whenever Big Al's Uncle Fred came for a visit, that phrase was quite literal. Big Al's Uncle and Cousin (John) trained wild animals to perform stunts in movies and in the circus, so, they would travel all over the US, picking up these animals from docs everywhere. Whenever Uncle Fred and John would come to Big Al's house, they would bring along these animals.

To say Big Al's house was total insanity during those visits would be an understatement. There were baby alligators in bathtubs. There were cages of all different kinds of animals all over the property. There were Rhinos in cages on the front lawn. Next to them were cages with Giraffes. There were tractor trailers everywhere, on the driveway and on the lawn.

Big Al's mom would take it all in stride, though. She didn't see the need to scream and yell or complain about how everyone was ruining her house. Afterall, it's not like she could stop the pandemonium anyway. And, deep down, she most likely enjoyed it, herself. There were many times, in the midst of all this chaos, that Big Al caught her with a smile on her face. And, on many occasions, when the entire family was around, she would join in on the laughter. In the end, the good times outweighed the craziness.

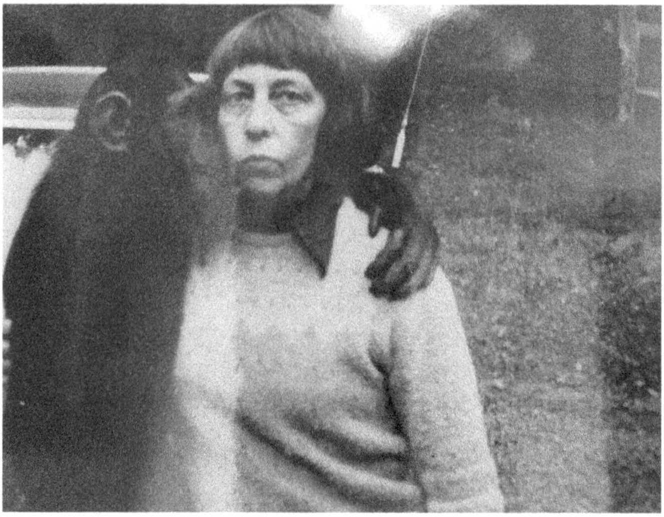

There was one animal that was more like a pet. Luckily for John, he resided in California, where it was legal to own certain wild animals. Even though Buddy the chimpanzee did perform stunts in movies and circuses, Buddy was a big part of the family. Buddy provided so much entertainment in the home, or wherever the family might be; he went everywhere with them. He was like a playmate that was always there, and up for anything.

One day, Big Al had a friend over, Chuck. It was a rainy summer day, and everyone was just hanging around the house.

They were goofing around with Buddy. Chasing him throughout the house, wrestling with him, etc. During one of those wrestling matches, Chuck and Big Al found themselves racking buddy; Chuck holding his feet and Big Al holding his arms. When Chuck and Big Al finally let go, they knew that Buddy would continue the fight, but they were surprised when what happened *actually* happened. Buddy got up, did a complete 180, and chased Big Al into the kitchen. Big Al ran so fast that he knocked the kitchen door off its hinges!

Buddy chased Big Al all the way out the back door. Chuck was laughing uncontrollably, (so much so that there was no way he could even try to help Big Al.) Big Al's mom, on the other hand, did not find the situation very funny; at first, she was in such shock that she just stood there with her mouth open, speechless; but once that shock passed, her calm, loving side was nowhere to be found. She went berserk, yelling at the boys and how they're going to ruin her house, screaming, "Fred, what are we going to do?!." Eventually, though, Big Al's mom did find the humor in the situation, and they all started laughing. She was sure to tell the boys, however, "the rough housing needs to stay outside from now on!"

BATHTIME FOR BUDDY

Every time it was time to bathe Buddy was an ordeal. Buddy hated the water, probably because chimps can't swim. But this time was made for the books:

Big Al and John needed to get Buddy all washed up after a day of playing in the mud and going to the local 7-11 where Buddy managed to get more of the chocolate and cream from the cream filled doughnuts all over his fur than in his mouth. Buddy, of course, was fighting them every step of the way. Finally, Big Al and John managed to get Buddy into one of the bathtubs in Big Al's home and got him all soaped up.

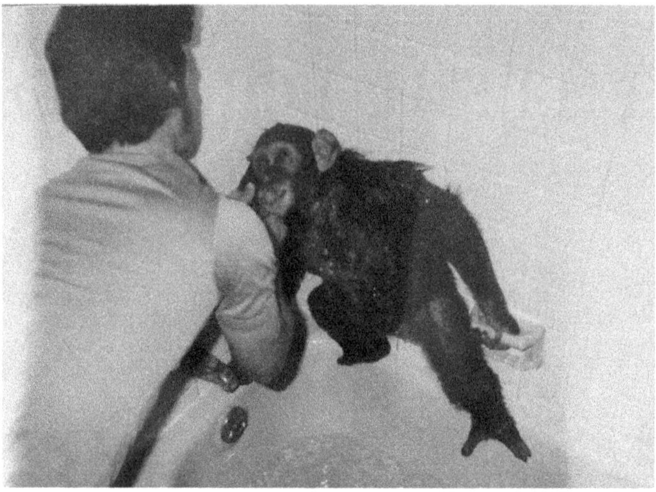

Even though Buddy could be a handful at times, Big Al loved to play with Buddy and tried to get the better of him all the time. Sitting on the bathroom sink next to the tub was a toy alligator. Big Al knew he would startle Buddy a little with what he was planning, but he did not expect the reaction that he got. Once Buddy was calm enough for Big Al to have a free hand, Big Al grabbed the toy alligator and dunked it under the water before anyone, Buddy or John, could notice. Slowly he peeked the little alligator's head out and crept it closer towards Buddy. Buddy was focused on John washing him and wasn't paying much attention to Big Al. When Buddy finally spotted that toy out of his side vision his reaction was priceless. He jumped out of the bathtub, pinning himself between the walls of the bathtub with his arms and legs like a tension bar. The expression on his face was priceless, as well; who would have thought that such a strong specimen could be so frightened of a little toy! Buddy was covered from head to toe with soap bubbles. He could only defy gravity for so long, though. Once he did start to slide down, he refused to go into that water again. He managed to push off one wall and land on the dry floor, feet first. Buddy starts to run around the small bathroom, screeching, flailing his arms, soap flying everywhere, tearing the towel rack right off the wall, and breaking it in half. Finally, Big Al and John caught him, and were able to wrap him in the towel. Buddy finally calmed down enough so that Big Al and John could actually get him dried off.

In that very moment, Big Al's mom came home and passed by the bathroom. She just gave Big Al and John a look that the boys understood in an instant. The two spent the rest of their day wiping up soap and water all over the bathroom walls, floor, just everywhere. They were able to fix the holes in the wall from the towel rack being torn off, but they couldn't repair all the damage; Big Al turned to John, "well, I guess we're going shopping for a new mirror and towel rack tomorrow."

LET'S PLAY

It's 1976, and one of Big Al's favorite pastimes is playing baseball; he pitches for his town's team, Babe Ruth. Big Al is a left-handed pitcher, and the team loves it; they all think that they have an advantage when Big Al pitches because the other team's batters are used to the pitch coming from a different angle, as well as making it more difficult for batters to anticipate the style of pitch.

So, it's bottom of the 6th, Big Al pitches a slider, the hitter hits a ground ball, it rolls right back to Big Al, Big Al throws it to Craig, his first base teammate. Craig catches it, swings around to tag the runner out, and *accidentally* hits him in the face. Well, the runner takes it as an intentional hit, and starts screaming at Craig, "what the hell, you son of a bitch." Craig say, "hey, calm down, it was an accident." The runner doesn't believe him and starts swinging at Craig. Well that's a mistake, because a simple misunderstanding soon turns into an all-out brawl. The runner's brother, almost immediately, races down from the bleachers and starts beating on Craig. Craig, of course, fights back. This goes on for about 2 minutes with the referees trying to break it up. Finally, the coaches come down, and break it up. The runner went back to his dug out, his brother went back to his seat, and Craig went back to first plate. All seemed to have calmed down, and back to game-time. It may have ended at that, but Big Al was involved.

At this point everyone is back to their positions, and the game is ready to restart. Big Al calls a time out before his pitch, walks over to Craig, and just says "get ready". Craig knew that Big Al wouldn't be able to just let what just happened go, so he wasn't too surprised that Big Al was up to something, but he wasn't sure what. He just thought, as did everybody else on the team, that Big Al would throw a wild pitch and hit the batter.

Big Al goes back to the mound, gets into his pitching stance, and fires one away - right into the other team's dugout! Since Big Al was left-handed, his pitching stance naturally had him facing their dugout, so they never suspected any foul play.

The ball bounces off the walls like a ping pong ball. Well that was it; everyone went crazy; the players from the opposing team come charging out of the dugout. Big Al's teammates come flying out of their dugout to join their teammates on the field, even the people from the stands (brothers, sisters, dads...), got involved. Everyone starts throwing punches, yelling and screaming at each other, there's gloves flying everywhere as well as bats. No one got seriously injured, but this was not a small brawl that could be broken up by the coaches and referees only. Ten minutes go by, and suddenly, "Waaaaaahhhhhhh, Waaaaaahhhhhhh, Waaaaaahhhhhhh…" and in come the police to intervene.

Finally, after 10 more minutes, the police were able to get the situation under control, but the game was never finished. The police insisted that everyone return to their vehicles, the game was over! Big Al and his teammates load up into the bus that they came in. The bus even got a Police escort back home. On the bus ride home, Big Al's coach said, "who thinks to throw the baseball into the dugout! I would have expected you to take retaliation on the batter, but I didn't even know how to respond to what you did!" Not only was that game never finished, or made up, but Big Al's team never played that team ever again!

FREEDOM

The first day of spring. Somehow, this spring sun felt warmer than others before it. Senior year in High School may have had something to do with that. Big Al and some friends decided to go dirt bike riding through the nearby woods. But, of course, they had to add a little twist to the ride. To spice things up a little, Big Al suggested that they all go streaking. Without even another breath, Big Al stripped down to nothing but his helmet and boots. Everyone else followed suit. Then they all ran across the highway. Everyone driving by were stunned at first, but then just started honking and laughing.

When the boys were running back, they could not cross the median, they were trapped by the heavy flow of traffic. Everyone would slowdown, just enough to laugh and stare, but not let them pass. Finally, they got back to their bikes, where a cop was waiting for them. The cop and the boys just locked eyes, but Big Al didn't give him any time to say anything. He just got on to his bike and slammed on the accelerator. Mud flying everywhere, including up Big Al's (back!)

Once Big Al got home and searched the pockets of his jeans that he was holding, he realized that his wallet was missing. His heart started racing; the cop never caught him, but what if he found his wallet at the scene? Big Al raced back to where he took off his clothes, hoping and praying the whole way. He found that his wallet was just sitting under the leaves. It must have slipped out as he was stripping.

As Big Al turned to get back onto his bike and head home, he bumped into another surprise; the mom of one of his High School friends'. The two of them had a very pleasant conversation about school and such. At the end of their conversation, as she was walking away and Big Al was getting back onto his bike, she turned, "by the way, the helmet and boots, nice touch", she said with a smile-she had been driving on the highway during Big Al's streaking adventure!

GOTCHA!

EASTER - a holiday without all the Pomp and Circumstance; nothing like Christmas or the Fourth of July. Still, with Big Al around, there are sure to be some fire works!

This story starts with Big Al and his friend Greg going to visit a mutual friend who had just returned from the Marines. Tom, the friend they were visiting, had trained with Big Al for years. Big Al and Greg wanted to welcome their friend home.

Big Al, Greg, Tom, and Tom's parents went out for dinner. The conversation for most of the night was filled with a lot of good stories and a lot of laughter. Tom's dad was in the Marines a few years back, as well. He was also in the Navy Reserves at the time. Mr. Smith would constantly brag about how his training was so intense, and how he was always aware of his surroundings. At dinner, the conversation turned to hypothetical situations, and how each person would deal with them. When a hypothetical kidnapping situation was presented, Mr. Smith was positive that something like that could never happen to him due to his training, and boasted about it throughout the conversation at dinner. So, Big Al and Greg gave each other a look, a look that said it all, and that's when the plan was hatched.

The following Friday, Greg called Big Al and asked what he had planned for the weekend. Big Al responds with "nothing special." There was a brief pause and then Greg proceeds to ask Big Al, "you thinking what I'm thinking?" Big Al then responds with, "let's go prank Mr. Smith!"

The next morning, Greg drove out, picked up Big Al, they talked about how they would execute their crazy plan, gathered all the gear they would need, and they were in South Jersey at the Smith house by Easter morning. They arrived when they knew everyone had gone to Church, and the house was empty. They brought with them a box which they had wrapped up like it was a package that had just been delivered. The box was meant to be a distraction for when the Smith's came home. They set it by the mailbox, knowing that Mrs. Smith would want to stop the car before getting to the house to grab it. Just in case that didn't work, a few feet further up the driveway they dragged a fallen tree to block the driveway. The tree was not huge, but it was enough so that the Smiths would need to stop the car so someone could move it. One way or another, that car was going to stop.

Big Al and Greg then hide in the bushes, on either side of

the driveway. They wait there for what seems to be an eternity. Finally, they hear the car coming up the long driveway (it looks more like a dirt road). Sure enough, the car starts to slow down to get the package from the mailbox. Mr. Smith had his window cracked a bit, and even though Big Al and Greg were very well hidden, they could still hear Mrs. Smith as she rolled down her window to retrieve the package, say, "oh, look, there's a package for Easter." As she starts to reach for the package, Big Al and Greg, in such stealthy, but speed of light fashion, jump out of the bushes. Big Al and Greg are in full disguise, there was no way any of the Smiths could tell who they were. Greg taps on the driver side window with his unloaded pistol and signals to Mr. Smith to get out of the car. At the time Mr. Smith was not aware that the pistol pointed at his head was not loaded, so he complied. At the same time, Big Al runs to Mrs. Smith's side and orders her to get out of the car. Big Al then tells her that all this is just half a joke/half training, but not to let on to Mr. Smith because in the end he would definitely appreciate this sharpening of skills exercise. He tells her to drive to the house and wait there. Big Al then hurries over so that he and Greg could carry out their mission. They tie Mr. Smith's hands, and his feet, leaving only enough length for him to waddle, "prisoner style", cover his mouth with duct tape, put a bag over his head, and lead him into the woods.

Big Al and Greg drag Mr. Smith through streams in his suit and tie, rough him up a little, and at some point, they even take his shoes so he's walking barefoot. Thirty minutes go by, walking through the rough ground, pushing through the thick brush. Finally, Big Al and Greg come full circle and make their way back to the house with Mr. Smith. As they come up to the front of the house, Mrs. Smith takes a picture, so they can all enjoy this later. Big Al and Greg then take their masks off and the bag off Mr. Smith's head.

Mr. Smith was speechless at first, a little disoriented, but everyone had a really good laugh. Once Big Al untied him, and Mr. Smith regained his composure and realized this was all a prank, he said, "wow you guys, you got me good! I do have to say, this was a real eye opener." He went on to tell them all how it was interesting how all his training really did come flooding back; he wasn't 100% sure that it would because he hadn't been in that type of situation for some time now. But when all the dust settled and everyone was sitting in the living room laughing, he said "remind me to NEVER tell you guys anything again!"

THE COVER UP

After dinner one night, Big Al, his mom and his dad were just sitting around talking, when suddenly, they hear a knock at the door. They weren't expecting anyone, and they seldom got visitors at this time of the night, so they were just a little taken aback. When Big Al opened the door, there was a man standing there who introduced himself as Steve. Steve said, "I'm so sorry, but I think I may have hit your dog. I was driving on one of the nearby roads and a Doberman Pincher just ran right in front of me. Your house was the closest around, so I thought maybe the dog was yours."

Right before dinner, Big Al had let Tracey, his black Doberman Pinscher, outside, so it was very possible that what Steve said was true. Big Al and Steve walked back down to the road. The state police arrived at that time. Sure enough, the dog was Tracey; she didn't usually come down to the road, but she did tonight. Steve just kept on about how sorry he was, and that it was an accident. Big Al just told him, "hey, don't worry about it, it's not your fault."

Big Al told the trooper that he would just carry the dog to the house and then take him straight to vet. The Trooper says, "I'll give you a blanket but it's got the State Police emblem on it, so just bring it back to the station when you're done with it." The Trooper goes to the back of his car, opens his trunk, and in it was a navy-blue blanket. Embroidered on the blanket was a triangle in yellow stitching, and inside the triangle were the words 'State Police', in the same yellow stitching. When the trooper goes to fluff out the blanket, a handgun falls out and slides right at Big Al's feet!

Given how this handgun was in the trunk, as if the Trooper did not want anyone to know about it, he probably shouldn't have been carrying it in his patrol car. Most likely, if his superiors got wind of this, he'd be in a very sticky situation. Big Al and the Trooper just stare at this weapon just lying there in the street, then stare at each other, and then the Trooper says, "if you didn't see that then you could keep the blanket." Big Al gives the Trooper a head nod and a little smirk, as if to say, "ok." In one felt swoop, the Trooper picked up the weapon, threw it in back of his car and drove off, not too fast, but fast enough to get the hell out of there. Big Al just stood there for a second, stunned. The Trooper took off so quickly, it was like watching a comedy show.

After a second past, Big Al just turned, picked up the injured dog, walked to his car, and went to the vet's. And that's how he got a cool 'State Police' blanket.

SURPRISE!

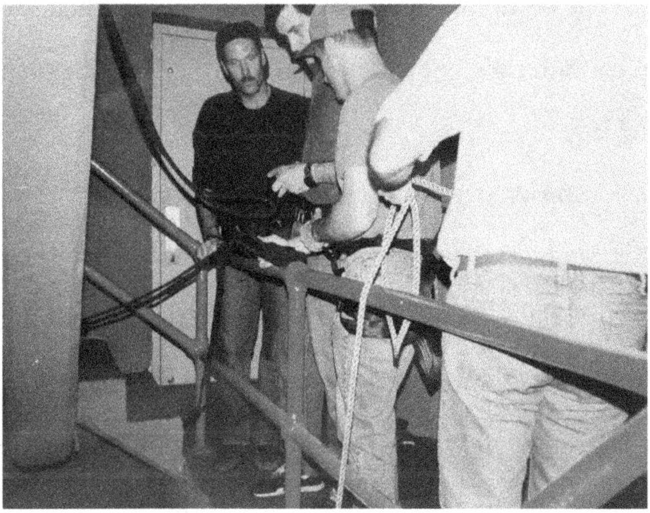

A few years ago, Big Al was training a DEA agent, Ted, in Martial Arts, as well as other survival techniques. One day during a Martial Arts lesson Ted and Big Al discussed other scenarios, and repelling came up. Ted worked in a 10-story DEA building, and suggested he and Big Al use it for their repelling training, if Big Al was willing to travel.

Big Al ordered the gear Ted and he would need, and planned on going to the DEA building as soon the order came in. The order arrived on a Wednesday, so they planned to go repelling on that Sunday. Since it was a Sunday, they didn't think anyone was there. When they went up to roof, they realized that the ropes they had ordered weren't long enough. That wasn't going to stop Big Al. Ted and Big Al went inside to the stairwell. The stairs hugged the walls as you ascended all the way up to the 10th floor. The ropes reached to the 6th floor, so they would repel down, then walk back up. Even though they got to repel inside, that was just practice for the real thing.

Big Al reordered the correct size ropes needed to scale the building, then he and Ted went back another Sunday. They waited until it was dark, so that it would be more challenging. As Big Al is repelling down the side of building, some guy goes to open the window on the 8th floor, working on a Sunday for some reason, messing up Big Al's plans! The guy looks at Big Al with this look of shock, fear, and confusion, all in one. Big Al thought this guy was going to pull out a gun and shoot him. Big Al thinks to himself, "how the hell do I handle this situation, I'm just hanging here."

Once the guy assesses the situation a bit more, and gains his composure, he turns to whoever else was with him and says, "there's someone fucking repelling the building." Then the guy turns back to Big Al and says, "are you fucking crazy, this is a DEA building full of guns and officers ready to shoot!" Ted, the agent that Big Al was training, knew the guy, yells up to him, "hey it's me" The guy turns around and yells to Ted, "what the fuck are you doing?!" Ted responds, "we're repelling. You want to join?" The guy responds with a simple "Fuck NO!!!!" The guy closes the window.

Big Al and Ted are thinking "ok we better get out of here now." They both rush down the rope as fast as they could from the 8th floor. They must have set a world record for speediest rope repelling. Low and behold, the adventure never ends, as soon as Big Al's feet hit the ground a prostitute comes up to him and propositioned him-it's pretty late already, and all the eccentrics of the city are out. Big Al just starts thinking to himself, "it doesn't even phase her that I just came off the side of a building."

The following morning, the director of Ted's division, was holding their usual meeting for all the agents and said, "There seems to be a few people who want to do training on their own time, but how about we keep the training that happens in this building Monday through Thursday 8:30am-6:00pm." Well, Big Al and Ted never did their repelling again-not at that building anyway.

LET IT SNOW

1977, Senior year in High School. Even the cold, cold winter couldn't get Big Al down. Not only was it Senior year, but Big Al had made it his life's mission to make the most out of each moment.

Big Al, Mark, and Chuck had been friends for years. They all lived near one another and were all in their last year of high school together. They would always walk to school together and were determined to make it the best year yet. They usually got to the school before the first bell rang and would just hang out in the courtyard outside the school, conspiring about ways to have a good time. On this particular day, though, their typical routine would need to change a little. It had snowed the night before and there were piles of snow everywhere. Big Al and his buddies couldn't play their usual basketball game, but that wasn't going to stop them from having fun. Big Al did not see the piles of snow as an inconvenience, or anything but an opportunity for some entertainment.

What started out as a snowball fight between friends just goofing around, soon turned into something else. Big Al didn't think it was right to keep the fun all to himself and his close friends, he wanted to share his joy with a larger group. So, the three got to talking and decided that they would liven up first period of day, bookkeeping.

Mr. Yutz, the teacher, had an odd phobia of open windows and closed them whenever he saw one. The room, 218, was on the second floor, right next to the courtyard. Students would constantly open the windows in class right before he got to the room, just to get his goat; he would come in, set his books down on his desk, then go close the windows; it was a tradition of sorts.

According to the plan that the boys hatched, Chuck and 2 of his friends would stay on the courtyard and prepare while Big Al and Mark went to class and set up for the prank on Mr. Yutz. The plan was for Big Al and Mark to open the windows, knowing that Mr. Yutz would close them, and the three boys that stayed back would pelt him with snowballs. Well, when Big Al went over to open the first window, he saw a line of at least twenty boys, snowballs in hand, and a pile in front of them for reloading. The three boys that Big Al had recruited to join in, did some recruiting of their own.

Of course, there were those who were not in on the prank who complained of the cold when the windows were opened. When Mr. Yutz comes in and sees the open windows in the middle of winter, he starts to huff and puff, and this time *slams* the books he's carrying onto his desk. As he walks over to shut the windows, he thinks to himself, 'these kids, will they ever stop!' Big Al turns to Mark, and in a soft voice says, "you might want to get down." Next thing you know, snowballs come flying in, one right after another. It was like a mini gun firing snowballs into the classroom. Those boys had some good arms because those snowballs were whipping in. All the other students were screaming and yelling, but Big Al was laughing so hard, taking cover under his desk. With Mark and Big Al laughing so hard, Mr. Yutz knew they were the instigators and sent them to the office. They got into some major trouble, but it was worth it! From that day on Mr. Yutz always made the boys close the windows!

ROUTE 287

This story takes place during the late 1970's when the traffic on Route 287 was very light. Big Al's friends, Chuck and Mark, lived nearby; Big Al and Chuck lived on one side of Rt. 287, and Mark lived across the highway in the woods. They had carved out trails on either side, and at night they would drag race on those trails, and cutting through Rt. 287, with their dirt bikes. The three boys waited until dark, the later, the better it seemed to make the experience, and they would mark off a section of the highway. Two of them would race while the other would wave the flag, and then they would switch. It was relatively easy to see if there were any other cars coming considering that there was hardly anybody on the road, and one would see their headlights.

The race would start at Mark's house, the boys would race the half mile of the woods until they reach the highway, then continue the race on Rt. 287 for a quarter of a mile, then curve back onto the other side of the road into the woods, continue another quarter of a mile, until they reached the finish line in the trail by Big Al's house.

On this night a State Police car was cruising Rt. 287. It had parked, lights off, on the shoulder, right where the boys would be racing out of the woods and onto 287. The officers did not expect to see any action that night, so when Big Al and Chuck came whizzing by, imagine their surprise. Soon enough, the cruising turned into a chase. Lights go on, sirens go on, Big Al drives as fast as he can into the woods and tries to hide his bike, under the leaves. Chuck on the right side of, but a little behind Big Al and the police. So, when the police car tries to follow Big Al, it cuts off Chuck. Chuck slams into the side of the police car with his bike, flies over the handles and rolls on the ground. Chuck doesn't get badly injured, but the policemen come out of their car ranting and raving. By now Big Al comes running back to the scene. Mark heard the commotion but took off and retreated into his house in fear of the consequences. As soon as the officers assess the situation and realize that Chuck is ok, they start screaming, "what the hell are you guys doing, are you crazy?!" Big Al thought for sure they would be spending the night, if not longer, in jail! In the end, though, the officers admit that the only reason that wasn't going to happen was because of the incident of the police car accidentally hitting Chuck.

THE FAST FIVE

12:00PM, Northern NJ - There's nothing left of the snow fall from two days ago except a dusting here and there. The sun is shining bright; and even though the air is crisp, it's been remarkably warm and sunny for the month of December. The sky looks like a painting in the museum- vital blue with just two or three perfectly formed clouds in just the right place. Big Al looks out his window and sees five cars lined up on his lawn on the side of his house. All these cars were older models; there were no SUVs or modern-day sports cars. They all looked like they've been in accidents, through a war zone, really- graffiti painted all over them, each one used for target practice, and all of them missing windows. None looked as if they would even start. But their engines did have one last run in them. Big Al was excited, because it was only a matter of two hours before his friends arrived, and the biannual Demolition Derby would begin!

Four of Big Al's friends would meet at Big Al's house and they would use the wooded area of the property located behind the home for the motor sport. All five guys would race the beat-up cars one last time and then send them off to the junk yard. To make the race a little more interesting, because the demolition of cars just wasn't interesting enough for these guys, they would use paint ball guns to shoot at each other as they raced around. Sometimes the paint ball pellets would hit the car itself, with just enough force to rattle and distract the driver, leaving room for one of the other guys to ram into the distracted drivers car at just the right angle, and eliminate him from the game; most of the time the driver of the targeted car would get a shot in the shoulder; but every once in a while somebody got struck in the head. Even with a helmet on, that stung! There were only 2 rules- 1. No head on collisions; most of time the guys drove in reverse; they would back into each other preserving the cars engines and limiting injuries. AND rule #2. No blasting anyone with the paintball guns for an hour. After that hour, all the guys would drive their cars to a centralized gathering place, stop, give each other a look that meant, "game on", then proceed to chase each other, shoot their paintball guns, and continue to try to eliminate as many other players as possible by rendering the other vehicles inoperable, and it was game over for that guy!

The guys Big Al, the brains of the operation; Mark Wilson; Harry Wilson; Chuck Davis; and Bobby Gibbs. Bobby was a used car salesman, but not the typical type you might think of. Bobby would always be scouting out cars that he could buy for cheap, $50-$100, fix them up, give them a new paint job, shiny up the engine, and then sell them for a profit. He would also be on the lookout for ones that the guys could use for their Demolition Derby. Once they collected 5 of these cars, they were good to go.

One day Bobby was going to meet up with a man named Doug who wanted to get rid of his broken-down Ford and wanted to buy the newer Ford that Bobby had just fixed up. Bobby owned a car lot in Hackettstown, not too far from Big Al, so he and Big Al drove in Big Al's car to meet Doug. Once they got there, they waited a while until finally Doug showed up. Bobby gets out of the car, puts his briefcase containing all the vehicle information on top of Big Al trunk, takes the paperwork out, and walks over to greet Doug. Doug asked, "how much?" Bobby wanted $1500. Doug proceeds with, "I'll give you $500." Bobby reminds Doug that they had agreed on $1500 over the phone. Doug and Bobby argue back and forth on price. Finally, Bobby says, "I'll smash this car before I sell it to you for $500." Doug made a sarcastic remark, "no way would you do that", and doesn't budge from price. Bobby, being Bobby, says, "o.k"; he then hands the papers to Big Al, and gets into the car that he and Doug were discussing. Big Al and Doug look at each other as to ask, "What is he doing?" Big Al knew, Doug didn't. Bobby starts up the car, speeds away, slams the breaks after about 10 feet, and T-bones into another car of his that is parked on the lot, making sure to keep both engines intact. Bobby gets out of that car, walks to Big Al, grabs the papers, puts them in the briefcase, all without saying a word. Still not saying anything, Bobby proceeds to get into drivers' side of Big Al's car, Big Al gets into passenger side, and they drive off. Doug is just standing there with his mouth wide open in disbelief. When Bobby breaks his silence, he turns to Big Al and says: "Well, we have 2 more cars to use in our demolition derby now!"

2:00PM - Time for the games to begin. All the guys were at Big Al's and ready to play, they all get their protective gear on. They all get their paint ball guns. You could hear all the engines rev up. From out of his car door window, Big Al counts down with his left fingers - ***3,2,1***. All five cars start racing, trying to avoid any obstacles that may be in the way. Even though this was an area of the woods that wasn't thick with trees or rocks, or whatever, one could always encounter a hurdle in one form or another in the path. Dirt and mud started spewing all over. Harry didn't even make it to the paintball portion of the race. His brother Mark, no less, took him out in forty-five minutes. Mark rammed Harry's car right into a tree, hard enough so that Harry's engine wouldn't start again. Once the paintball part commenced, each player followed Harry one by one. Whether they wound up in a ditch, or just because the car was rammed hard enough where the engine gave out.

3:30PM - Only 2 guys left- Bobby and Big Al. Bobby fired his paintball gun with amazing accuracy right though the opening of the back windshield and blasted Big Al right in the back of his head so that Big Al was stunned enough to drive over a tree stump. Big Al's car was stuck. Bobby comes around the corner, stares straight at Big Al, they lock glares for a moment, you could hear Bobby rev up his engine. Big Al quickly unfastens his seatbelt and moves over to the passenger seat, and then Bobby T-bones Big Al right in front of his driver's side door. Because Bobby hit the car at just the right angle, so close to the engine, Big Al's car catches fire! Big Al was able to get out, then he and all the guys run to the shed to grab some buckets, then quickly fill them with water from the nearby pond, dumping them onto the car, in an attempt to put out the fire. Unfortunately for the five friends, their attempts were in vain. Now the car was engulfed in flames, and Big Al's neighbor's tree catches fire. Being that the guys didn't have just a small fire on their hands anymore, they then come to realization that they need to call fire company. These guys were either firemen or cops themselves just having fun, but they knew they didn't have the equipment needed for the job.

3:45PM – Everything was nice and quiet at the Firehouse; not much activity on a Sunday. Suddenly, the siren signaling an emergency sounds. Now the air is full of energy; all the firemen are rushing to get their gear on, they all hear the dispatcher telling them the address, and they drive the firetruck out of the station with the emergency lights on. The two Police officers that reported to the scene at Big Al's house were astonished by what they were seeing. They see an out of control fire, that they feared the firefighters wouldn't be able to get out before it spread, they see Big Al and his four friends dressed in camo, shot up with paint ball paint, and they see cars scattered throughout the yard looking even worse. The Fire company finally gets the fire out, before it traveled any further. The neighbor's tree was destroyed, but the neighbor didn't care. The one officer asked if Big Al had the registrations for these vehicles. Big Al's response, "Hell no, we're just using them one last time, and then we're junking them right afterwards." The explanation seemed reasonable enough, but the 2 cops just look at each other for a moment with bewildered looks on their faces. One of them finally says, "how the hell are we supposed to write this one up?"

4:30PM – Now the sky looks like it's on fire with the setting sun; it was a bright orange with brilliant red streaks. The car/tree fire was out, but the fire department was still there cleaning up, and the Police were still there. In comes Bruce, a friend of Big Al and Bobby, with his car crusher and flatbed. One by one, he loads the junk cars onto the crusher so that he could drop them off at the junkyard. Once all five cars are flattened and on the flatbed, he gets in the driver seat ready to drive off, turns to Big Al and says, "you know I'm going to get a whole bunch of questions as to why I'm showing up with these cars that look like they just came out of a war zone." Big Al just hands Bruce $100 and says, "just take the cars."

The next day, 11:00AM - Word of the incident traveled back to Big Al's friend in the Police department, so Big Al gets a call from him the next day. All he had to say was, "you guys might want to lay low for a while and put off your next demolition derby, and please stop setting fires!"

"MORE PLEASE!"

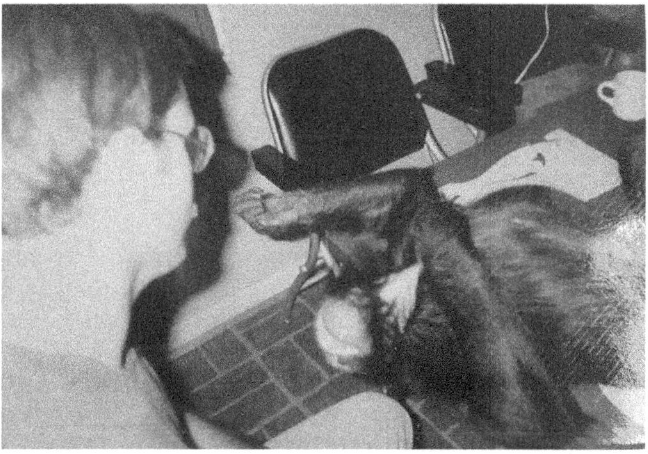

It's 4th of July in Far Hills, 5pm. Big Al was planning to go to the annual fourth of July fair, located in Chester, NJ, with two of his friends, Brian and Chuck. The three boys were heading over to enjoy the festivities before the 9:00pm firework display, but Big Al could not just settle for just the norm. He decided to unleash some excitement of his own that night, but it turned out to be a little more than he bargained for.

One of Big Al's other buddies, Tom, had just come home from the military. Tom couldn't make it to the fair that night, but Big

Al was sure to bring the present that Tom had brought back with him- two smoke Grenades! As Big Al, Brian, and Chuck drive off and onto 287, Big Al holds one of the smoke grenades out his window, then drops it to ground. There are no cars on the exit ramp behind them, so no one ran the risk of being blinded. The air fills up with purple smoke. The three friends drive away, thinking nothing of it, besides 'wasn't that cool.' Seconds later, they hear on the CB radio Big Al installed in his car, "Breaker 1-9, fire on 287 exit 13." The boys just looked at each other, and then pulled onto the shoulder.

All the firefighters, including the ones from Far Hills, had already gathered for the big fourth of July fair in Chester. But they, of course, had their radios on listening for the operator to pull them away at any time. All was quiet for over an hour now, and the men thought they were in the clear for a while, so they all started to relax a bit. The calmness didn't last for long, though. They all hear the dispatcher calling someone to Exit 13 on 287. The designated firefighters responsible for answering the call that round gathered onto the firetruck, changed into their fire gear as quickly as they could, and raced to the scene. After making the 15 minute drive to the scene, they all look at one another thinking 'did we get the location wrong- there's no fire here.' In that moment one of the firefighters looks over to the car stopped on the shoulder up ahead. He signals to his colleagues and walks over to see if the boys standing there knew anything about the supposed fire. When he gets closer, he sees Big Al and his friends laughing. He says, "I would never wish for a fire, but please don't tell me that this call was some kind of prank."

Big Al explained that he and his friends meant no harm; they did not expect the fire company to be called; the smoke was minimal, and it disappeared in 10 minutes. The firefighter laughed, then he turned to Big Al and said, "you know, things were just starting to get good over there, they were just about to open the kegs;" then he chuckled, "let's go", and they all rode over to the fair, Big Al's car following the firetruck.

CAMPING OUT

Another moment with Big Al: It's late March on a Friday. Big Al's High School experience would soon come to an end, so he wanted to make the most out of his time. He knew that soon reality would hit, and care-free weekends would become more and more scarce. The weekend ahead looked to be very warm with no rain in sight, according to the forecast; not that bad weather would ever stop Big Al, though. Big Al and his buddy Chuck decided to go camping that weekend. They had packed the night before, so as soon as the dismissal bell rang, they would drive to Mine Mountain, where they would start their three-day adventure. They started off by hiking at Mine Mountain for about an hour, and then they decided it was time to make camp for the night before they lost too much light. The flashlights they brought were bright, but nothing could beat the light of day. The boys had timed it just right, too; by the time the sky turned that golden reddish hue of the setting sun, they were already sitting by their campfire, eating their dinner. The rest of the night was spent swapping stories, and with a little exploring with flashlights not too far away from campfire. Soon it was time to get some sleep; after camping that night at Mine Mountain, they would make their way to other nearby hiking opportunities.

The two found a good spot, far away from any other people who may be camping out; their campsite was in the woods, in a clearing about ½ a mile from the highway. Being so close to the highway did present one, *unforeseen* problem, though; as the fire started to die down, the smoke became more intense. At 2:00 that morning Big Al was wakened from his sleep to the blaring sound of sirens. The long, droning sounds were coming from up and down the highway. At first, he had no clue what's going on, so he walked a little closer in hopes that he would hear something that would alert him to what the bustle was about. He did hear firefighters yelling to one another that smoke had been spotted by a motorist driving on the highway, called it in, and now the crew needed to pin-point where the source was. From what the firefighters were yelling to one another, Big Al was able to conclude that they were looking for a possible forest fire. He runs back to his campsite and tells Chuck - "Chuck, the whole damn fire company is out there, and I think they're looking for us." Chuck says, "What!", and he halls ass deep into the woods, and just leaves Big Al to deal with any backlash!

As they follow the smoke, the firefighters finally run into Big Al. Big Al acts totally dumbfounded, and just asks them what's going on. They explain that they were following smoke that would possibly lead them to a forest fire. Then one of the firemen looked over Big Al's shoulder, sees Big Al's campfire 50 feet away, and proceeds to question Big Al a little more: "Are you camping? You know, there's a designated spot for camping a couple of miles that way." Big Al just shrugged his shoulders. The Firefighter instructed Big Al to follow him. They kept walking in the direction of the campfire. When they finally reach the campfire, the firefighter instructed Big Al to wait there. The fireman continued a little further into the woods to ensure that what he suspected was true - the campfire was the cause of the commotion! When the fire fighter felt confident that his original suspicion was correct, he yelled out to all the other firefighters, “don’t worry guys, it’s just a campfire!” The men were not happy about being dragged out of their beds at 2 in the morning for a campfire, but all in all, they all had a good laugh at the bizarre situation.

FIRECRACKER FRIDAY

Senior year in High School, the year every student longs for, and Big Al was no different. He was, however, determined to be remembered after his four-year tenure, so he and his friends were always up to "extracurricular" activities during school hours. The year of 1977, Big Al's senior year, though, the stakes seemed higher, so Big Al made sure he'd go out with a bang!

It's the last period of the day, on a Friday. Even with the colder than usual April day and the misty weather, everyone was looking forward to the weekend, but no one expected that it would start in the next 10 minutes, before the last bell of the day would ring. Big Al, along with three of his friends were in their study hall. Down the hall was their target, the advanced math class. In that class was their friend Billy, and a lot of prim and proper girls who were soon to be very surprised. The boys' goal would be easier than expected, because the door to that class was left open. After many days of preparation, the fun was about to begin. Big Al, Russ, Marc, and Chuck had stocked Marc's Mustang with all kinds of firecrackers, Whistling Bottle Rockets, included. One by one, each would ask to use the rest room, but instead of going to the expected destination, they would head straight for the exit door at the end of the hallway which lead straight to Marc's car. Once they reached the car, the boy would retrieve as many firecrackers as he could hold in his pockets. Every pocket was full- jacket pockets, pant pockets, shirt pockets, (their preparation involved choosing the right clothes for the job, too.) As they re-entered the building from the same door, they each would strategically place the firecrackers along the hall, as well as on the staircase located by the exit/entrance door. When the last boy involved, Big Al, asks to use the restroom, he gathered his firecrackers from Marc's trunk, lined them up in the hallway and on the steps as planned, then he walked back towards the staircase as fast as he could without bringing attention to himself from the other classrooms along the hallway, lighting the fuses and ran out the back door again!

BOOM!, CRAKLE!, BANG! The hissing and whistling sounds came from every which direction. From outside the cracked door, Big Al lit and tossed even more firecrackers inside. Everyone in the targeted math class was startled, yelling, "OMG!", "what in the world is going on!", etc. But they weren't alone; every class in that hallway was affected, including the Study Hall. Seconds later, over the loudspeaker, the code was given for lock down of the entire school. As the Study Hall teacher rustled his students to the nearest class, the other three boys made their escape in the commotion out the back door to meet up with Big Al. They too joined in with tossing more firecrackers into the building. Once they were out of firecrackers, the four boys waited outside until the lockdown was over. Soon enough, administration figured out what caused the ruckus. The boys heard the ceased lock down announcement from outside, re-entered the building, and then heard Principle Wallus announce that all student had to line up by their lockers, as each locker was searched for any remaining firecrackers. There were none to be found, however, since Big Al, Russ, Marc, and Chuck had used them all. The principle and many of the staff knew who the culprits were, but there was no proof!

"SHOT ON GOAL!"

Another rainy, ugly Monday. It's only 11 am and the whole school day is still ahead. Last week was George Washington's birthday, but now there's not another break for at least another month! The school has now fallen back into its hum drum routine, a perfect time for Big Al to shake things up.

Big Al was in Mr. Beckham's 4th period English class. Mr. Beckham was a tall man, clean shaven; at first glance he seemed like a nice guy, but he was very strict when it came to his students. The entire student body disliked him. They would always talk about him behind his back, especially about how he would jump at every little thing. The consensus was that Mr. Beckham was so on edge all the time because he used to play goalie on a hockey team, and it was just a knee jerk reaction. All the students knew that no matter what they did, each time they entered Mr. Beckhams class, they were in for a hard time. Today, though, he was even more overbearing, so Big Al thought, 'ok, I'll get back at him one day.' After English class was lunchtime. During lunch Big Al and some other guys were talking about how Mr. Beckham was even more harsh today, and they all decided that he deserved a little pay back, but at that point it was all just talk.

A week goes by, and, by request of his mother, Big Al is tasked with cleaning out the garage. During this undertaking, he discovers some old sports gear which had accumulated over the years- a couple of baseball mitts, a few soccer balls, and amongst it all were about 12 pucks from his hockey playing years. Those hockey pucks gave Big Al an idea; after all, he couldn't let those pucks go to waste, could he? So, the following day, Big Al brings a bunch of hockey pucks to school. He wasn't too sure what he was going to do with them, yet, but he knew he'd come up with something for Mr. Beckham. The guys that Big Al was talking with last week wanted in on the prank, so they devised a plan.

The day goes on as usual; Mr. Beckham was his usual stern self when the guys had him in 4th period English class, but right after lunch, the guys are ready to unleash their plan. It was 5th period. Mr. Beckham was preparing to start his next class. Big Al retrieved the pucks from his locker. Once Mr. Beckham's classroom door was closed, most of the guys lined up next to each other, in front of the entrance; all but one-Mike's job was to open the door when he heard the signal from Big Al. Mike finally heard, "Shot on goal!" Mike opens the classroom door, and all the others fling the puck into the room, aiming right at the board! All the students in the class were shocked, but Mr. Beckham's reaction was priceless. "Holy Shit!"; hearing that coming from a teacher made getting in trouble worth it.

BRICKS

Big Al's Senior year. Excitement is in the air because graduation is very close. Some students are talking about what theme song will be chosen at the prom, or what outfit they'll be wearing, or planning decorations. Big Al and his buddies just want out, though.

Big Al is in Mrs. Delahanty's English class. It's time for her to pass out the graded writing assignment from the day before. Big Al knew he wasn't getting an "A", but he was surprised when Mrs. Delahanty handed him a paper with an "F." Well, Big Al didn't except that grade, "There is no way that I got an "F!" Mrs. Delahanty, "sorry, but yes you did." Big Al thought to himself, 'I at least wrote the thing, I should have at least gotten a "D".' Mrs. Delahanty started to walk away, continuing to pass out the rest of the papers, but before she could, Big Al crumbled the paper and threw it back at her face. Now, all the other students are just looking at him. He gets out of his desk, walks to the front of the room, pulls 2 free desks together. At this point, all eyes are still on him, wondering, 'what the hell is he doing.' Over on the windowsill was a makeshift bookcase made with patio bricks. Big Al walks to them, removes the books, grabs a brick, and places it on the inner edges of the desks that are slightly separated. He walks back to get another brick and put that one on top of the first. Everyone is still staring at Big Al, still wondering what he's up to.

Meanwhile, Big Al's buddy Matt thinks this is a signal for him to goof off; he goes to the front and does a headstand, just because. The whole class is really in astonishment now; 'What the hell is going on in here?!' With that Big Al hammer fists the bricks! Pieces shatter everywhere, the students observing this circus jump in their seats, Mrs. Delahanty jumps as well, and then she runs out of the room screaming to the principle.

Mrs. Delahanty wanted to kick Big Al out of English, but without that class, he wasn't going to graduate. Mr. Kennedy, one of the other English teachers, knew Big Al, and thought that this was just too harsh, so he offered to have Big Al transfer to his class. So, Big Al was able to graduate with his class, and the administration even said that his was the best graduating class ever. Every practice went smooth. All the kids listened to all the directions, and never questioned them. At the end of the day, graduating, and being free from high school was everyone's primary goal!

MR. TOUGH GUY, HUH?

It's 1974, freshman year of high school. Big Al was in his study hall with Chuck and 20 other kids. Some kids kept to themselves, just doing their schoolwork. Some kids hung out and just talked. And then there was William. He was very quiet, more so than the "norm", very socially awkward, and he had always shied away from conflict. There was one boy in that study hall that thought this made William "an easy target" and thought he would take advantage of that. So, this boy started saying not-so-nice things to William. Big Al asked him to stop, but he wouldn't. Another student said something, too, but this bully just kept on with his trash talking, totally ignoring everyone else.

Well, Big Al had enough, he grabbed the guy by the shirt, held him against the wall, and said, "you need to back the fuck off." Big Al let go of the kid, thinking that was the end of it. Twenty seconds later, the guy makes another snide remark towards

William. That was it, Big Al had enough. He grabbed the kid again, but this time he dragged him onto the stage, (study hall was held in the theatre at the far end of the high school). Big Al hog tied the kid, hands and feet behind his back.

Almost immediately, the bell rang for the next class. A period goes by, and now Big Al is in his Math class with Mr. Kennedy. On the intercom, "Mr. Kennedy, is Bobby Aldman in your class?" Big Al looks at Chuck, "they found him!"

Big Al got expelled for this one, and when his father came to get him from school, he thought for sure his dad was going to kill him. For the first ten minutes of the car ride home was silence, Big Al didn't dare say a word. But then his dad says, "ok, Bobby so let's hear *this* story." Big Al told his dad what happed. His dad just said, "oh, so some kid was picking on William?" When Big Al explained why he did what he did, the dad couldn't be angry; he may have handled the situation a little differently, but Big Al was only trying to defend William, so how could the dad be angry?

IT'S RAINING TYPEWRITER

Big Al, as you've probably already noticed, is such a character. He's always looking to get in a good laugh where he can. In High School, though, he was king of the pranksters.

In Typing class, the teacher, Mrs. Miller, assigned seats to her students alphabetically, according to their last names. She thought she was so clever starting from the back row of the room. Big Al sat in the very back row, next to the window. When the end of the marking period was close, Mrs. Miller always had her students tell her what they thought they deserved, then she would average it together with the grade SHE thought they deserved, and that would be their final grade. It became like a ritual of sorts. She would pass out blank sheets of paper, and each student would write down their name and their "grade", then pass the sheet up to the front. Now, in the whole marking period, Big Al was lucky if he even typed one word, but that didn't stop him from giving himself an "A."

Chuck, Big Al's buddy, sat in the front row but in same line as Big Al. When Chuck got Big Al's paper and saw the "A" written on it, Chuck looked at Big Al and said, "you can't give yourself a grade higher than mine", so he crossed it out an gave Big Al a "B".

The next day, when the end of marking period came, Mrs. Miller handed everyone their final grades. When Big Al saw "F", he was angry. "What the hell?!" He thought that if Chuck hadn't changed that grade from an "A" to a "B", at least he would have ended up with a "D." Then Mrs. Miller says, "I guess I'll be seeing you next semester", as she lets out a little giggle. Well, Big Al's anger turns right away off Chuck. "There's no fucking way I'm gonna take this class again!", he says. And with that, he crumbles the paper with the "F", and throws it right back at Mrs. Millers face. Mrs. Miller says, "I know you're upset, but you got an "F", and those are the rules." Big Al replies, "Oh, ok, so you're gonna give me an "F", huh?" And, still staring at Mr. Miller, Big Al grabs the big, black, bulky typewriter off his desk, holds it out the window, and drops it from the 2nd story window!

After a moment, Big Al realized, the smoking lounge was down below. He looked out the window to find five staff members that had gone to the designated smoking area, looking in astonishment at the typewriter that just exploded on the ground ten feet away. Then they all stare at him, "what the hell?" Then they look back at the pieces of what used to be a typewriter, still in total disbelief. A minute goes by, when, over the intercom, "Beeep….Bobby Aldman to the office, right now!" Once Big Al got to the principle's office, Mr. Wallus says to Big Al, "You through a typewriter out the window?!" Big Al replies, "yea, I can't get an 'F' and take typing again, I don't want to type, I HATE typing!"

The school decided that a two-day suspension was good enough punishment. It wasn't worth torturing Big Al and having him repeat the class. Not only would he be miserable but having him in class would not be beneficial for Mrs. Miller, either!

CPSIA information can be obtained
at www.ICGtesting.com
Printed in the USA
BVHW072011120720
583568BV00001B/129

9 781489 726568